D1508734

African Venus

African Venus

Sheryl K. Carkhum-Lord

Library of Congress Control Number:		2013905829
ISBN:	Hardcover	978-1-4836-1780-0
	Softcover	978-1-4836-1779-4
	Ebook	978-1-4836-1781-7

This book was printed in the United States of America.

Rev. date: 07/10/2013

To order additional copies of this book, contact:
Xlibris Corporation
1-888-795-4274
www.Xlibris.com
Orders@Xlibris.com
127997

For my mother and father, Edith and Curtis Carkhum

My grandparents, Louise and Russell Maceden

And my husband, Bruce K. Lord Jr.

Chapter 1

Sitting on his throne, King Ghezo could reflect on his eminent and complete domain. He could feel the power resonating from the skull heads of dead enemies that were at the base of the throne and felt even more empowered by the patchwork made from elephant ivory.

He was *sèmèdo,* master of the world; everything was within his reach. He had the power to send armies into neighboring lands to capture slaves or to work his palm-oil plantations and to use them as sacrificial victims in the annual custom ceremonies.

His Benin lands reached from the Atlantic Ocean in the south to all Nigeria, Niger, Burkina Faso, and Togo—the famed Gold Coast of West Africa. He was on a ruthless mission to increase his lands even further. His imposing figure stood tall over the meeting with his royal advisors. He was five feet five inches tall with an oval face that showed little emotion in public. His body was muscular and lean. He was a young ruler but learned much from his father about ruling.

His favorite wife was standing on the right side of him, and his mother stood on the left.

The discussion was held in the *kpodoji* courtyard and centered around the arrival of the first French delegation to the Royal Palace. The council members were planning the event, but the king looked preoccupied. He abruptly got up and left the area with his entourage in tow. Everyone was bowing uneasily in his wake, knowing full well they must work out every detail to his satisfaction.

He felt compelled to spend his afternoon among his many children and moved toward his wives' huts to surprise them. He looked forward to their squeals of joy and laughter as this was an unplanned visit.

As they gathered round him, he looked into each of his male children to see the reflection of the next king. *Which son will it be?* he thought. Should it be Glele or Ahkeose or Osadota? It was not a decision for today. Today he would just enjoy their company, and the company of his only daughter, Nima.

Several weeks later, the king received Admiral Versallies with a royal welcome and a show of his military prowess. His elite soldiers led them through the town of Kana and over the bridge to the Royal Palace of Abomey. The people lined the road, leading in waving colorful appliquéd banners. When they arrived at the courtyard, the female Amazon warriors were at the right of the king and his royal family and other dignitaries were at his left.

The French brigade proudly wore their woolen parade uniforms with country flag colors of red, white, and blue bellowing in the African heat. Even the horses were decorated with feathered headdresses.

After the welcome address, festive song and dance and drumming were performed; the gifts from one king to another were shown.

King Ghezo received bolts of golden cloth, a timepiece, and a fine military sword. To be presented to King Philippe were a baby elephant, raw diamonds, and slaves.

King Ghezo seemed most impressed by the French uniforms and spoke to the admiral.

"Tell your King Philippe thank you very much. But the next time you come, bring me uniforms like yours for my Amazons."

The admiral was taken aback by the request but nodded in agreement or compliance—he was not sure which.

"Certainly we will prepare our finest garments for your warrior women."

The azure sky stretched for miles about the golden city. The compound was busy with last-minute preparations for the wedding of Princess Nima of the royal Dahomean court, daughter of King Ghezo, to Prince Manko, son of General Mamboza. She had consented to marry the son of the second most powerful man in this tiny kingdom. The planning had begun two moons ago, with guests arriving from every corner of the Benin lands.

King Ghezo's palace residence was situated south of the entrance into the Royal Palace of Abomey. The current king would move through the *kpodoji* of one former king and the *ajalahennu* of another to arrive at his own *ajalala*. He could feel secure that not only his ancestors were watching but also the elite guards of the monarch, and the Dahomean female Amazon warriors were just across the courtyard. The back door of the a*jalala* led to the wives' huts as well.

The building was a one-story red earthen structure with several columns with openings decorated with the king's bas-relief symbol of power—the buffalo. It was the largest *ajalala* on the grounds and opened out to a great reception hall. The labyrinth of buildings included meeting places for royal business, including receiving foreign guests, and residences for the princesses. The structures were strong and would stand the test of time.

The palace was large and full of activities with markets and celebrations. On its periphery, it was six miles long and included high walls and dry mots filled with pinprick shrubs of the acacia plant. The palace was considered a fortress for the royal family and hard to penetrate by her enemies. Enemies like the Togolese and the Nigerians who would want to see King Ghezo pay for the many raids and stealing away of people, breaking up of families, and setting a course for years to come, supplying anyone who comes asking—be it the French, British, or Portuguese—with slaves.

Princess Nima had her hair twisted like rope and applied shea butter to her body, starting at her round forehead, down her arched eyebrows, across her nose and high cheekbones, down across her full lips to her square chin and firm neck. The scent relaxed her and felt good to massage into her skin. As she finished, her servants arrived, singing in a soft low tone.

Zaillia hummed the melody as she approached Nima. She had cared for and assisted her since her birth, and the two women began to hum together. Two other women followed Zaillia into the room. They bore the wedding garments and jewelry. The garment was splendid; Princess Nima had insisted on helping with its design. It was made out of traditional Adinka cloth with added gold beading. The gold jewelry, including bracelets and earrings, were exquisite as well. Tooled and fired by the best metalworkers of the court. These women wrapped and tucked the cloth around Nima's sixteen-year-old frame. Finally the last ceremonial headwear and rings were applied. The hour had arrived, and she was ready for her future husband.

As the wedding party began to assemble, King Ghezo thought not only of the future of his beloved daughter, but also of his monarchy. Yes, the French would bring many things to his kingdom of Dahomey. They would infect them with guns and bullets. They were not here to increase the holdings of King Ghezo and expand his lands. The king also knew they were not to be trusted. They were unlike the Arabs from the north or the Nigerians to the south; they came from much farther away. He was so preoccupied with thoughts about the intrusive Admiral Versallies, it almost distracted him from the festivities.

The meetings with Admiral Versallies were becoming more frequent and demanding. The French were not satisfied with slaves. They were like the dust of the desert, attempting to cling to everything in its path. He had disliked giving them so many slaves to ship off to their lands, but he disliked even more their request for rights of ports. They would not stop with this foothold. The king's thoughts brightened as the bridal party approached. This marriage would be a good alliance.

Chapter 2

King Louis Philippe was not satisfied with the borders of France. For years, he had been told about the African lands known as the Kingdom of Abomey in Benin. Confirmed were the stories of all-female regiments that were well trained and physically prepared, that these warrior women guarded the king and were held in high esteem throughout the land. He had also been brought samples of their metalworking skills, ranging from full-scale statues of people and animals to bas-relief plaques. Strategically, it was desired because it gave France access to the Cotonou Lagoon, a port that could bring slaves to French-dominated countries to work the land. Places like Martinique, Guadeloupe, and Saint Lucia needed plantation workers who could stand the heat and humidity of the tropics.

If the French government could not rule over its own people, it could certainly go elsewhere to dominate other people. And King Louis Philippe knew they were particularly good at doing that. They had the ships and the military talent to do it. No other European county had such far-reaching influence. King Louis

Philippe would be meeting with his military cabinet to discuss the unofficial focus of his regime. Infiltrate the land, dominate the people, steal their riches, and enslave them. Learn all about their ways and traditions, and use it to make their way into their lands. Use physical and psychological techniques to make that happen.

It was a lovely spring day at the Sun Place in France. Admiral Versallies had arrived with his entourage, prepared to meet with the king. He came from a long line of military men and knew of no other profession to put his efforts in. He had some other conquests under his belt, so he had no doubt that his presence was appreciated and his report would be well received. He had a round face with a long angular nose and a slightly jaunty chin. He had piercing black eyes and flat, wide mouth.

He would report that the *Lady Giselle* was ready to set sail to the Kingdom of Dahomey. The ship would leave this port fully stocked with supplies and food. They carried not only the necessities but a few additions like wine, cheese, live chickens, a goat, and the latest fishing gear. They knew how to capitalize the space on each level of the ship. And he was prepared to meet with King Ghezo. He would bring gifts sent to him on behalf of King Louis Philippe. King Ghezo had specifically pointed out how he would like uniforms for his Amazon women in the style of the French uniforms. So the presentation of those to him would be the highlight of the gifts.

The ship itself was beautifully designed to cut the water swiftly and gracefully. The billowing sails caught the sunlight, and the bow waited impatiently to be directed. The nautical equipment on board was the latest in scientific design, and the crew was made up of experienced seamen. The run from Nice, France, to Benin would be destined for success. Such a beautiful piece of boating equipment to be used for such a dubious cause. The *Lady Giselle* would handle the rigors of sea travel well. The French *barque* had four sails and was designed for maximum accommodations and safety. During her maiden voyage to Benin, she would encounter some strong headwinds near the Canary Islands and take on water. The well-trained crew would handle her with precision, making the passage from France to Africa in good time.

Chapter 3

The Yoruba military Chief Akuna was a thorn in the side of the Dahomean conquest. He seemed to be able to anticipate their every military maneuver and relished in it. He refused to let them raid any more villages under his command and called upon the powers of the occult to outsmart them. He developed a keen ability to position men in the right places.

Chief Akuna hated the arrogance of King Ghezo and never forgave them for stealing away so many of his beloved people, the Mahi. He was determined to have the upper edge against them.

Akuna was a tall and handsome man. His skin was a smooth, burnt, dark brown except for a keloid scar that was on his right arm, with piercing cowrie-shell-shaped ebony eyes. He was muscular in build, and his height of five feet eight inches made him tower over most of the men in his regiment. He was respected among them and desired by many women.

Of course, every man has his weakness and his pleasures. This chief returned from long travels always with a celebration and dancing in the streets. The young unmarried women on display in their colorful dresses danced to the beat of seduction.

So two Amazon warrior women were sent to seduce him. They became a part of the celebration and caught his attention. The twins were a novelty to him and a sign of good luck, so he had them both.

Perhaps it was the sway of their ornate grass skirts as they moved along the parade route or the dance that they performed in unison in his honor. That night, they were both in his chambers, and the two women were his match. When they left two days later, they took with them his edge. And things begin to change against his enemy. They seemed to outsmart his every move. His military astuteness was lost in the sexual escapade, and it would have to be regained at all cost. The French would become allies. They were always looking for information about the Fon. The day they arrived at his headquarters would prove invaluable in his pursuit of revenge. They would meet several times to develop a plan that would stun the great King Ghezo, his family, and his warriors.

The details of how they would enter the palace compound were finalized. The best time to do it was determined to be during the annual customs ceremonies. No one would suspect a kidnapping would take place then. The plan to penetrate the royal residence would take place after midnight when the fires are low and the watchmen would perhaps be drowsy. Drowsy or not, the slow and crocodile-like movements of the elite group of men sent in to do the task were organized and given exact instructions. The layout of the grounds and which side of the palace would be the best to approach were discussed. The first line of defense would be how to deal with the ditch of pin-sharp whistling thorn that surrounded the palace. A collapsible bridge was built to span over the ditch. Once all three men were over, they moved through the maze of small streets easily, bringing no attention to themselves. They were dressed like slaves of the household but had weapons within reach. All was quiet when they reached the sacrificial hut about five hundred yards from the gates to the king's palace. They had to move toward the far right and enter into the correct doorway. The right doorway was crucial because the *ajalala* of King Ghezo was known as the hall of many openings. But they knew exactly where they were going and who they were after. A member of the royal family was the paramount goal. The great King Ghezo would soon lose his beloved daughter. They knew she had just given birth to her first child and that it was a difficult birth. She was recovering and not able to go to the annual customs ceremonies. The household spy that they conferred with confirmed her location inside. In the middle bedroom, they would find her because colorful appliqué banners where displayed to celebrate the birth of her son.

They moved in swiftly, with one man staying near the entrance, and the other two men entered her room.

She was alone except for the sleeping baby. The room was dimly lit, but the warriors could see her outline, and the next thing that happened would take Nima from the world she loved to an unknown land and out of Africa.

The warrior took out his blowgun and blew a red feather dart into Nima. She stirred and moaned slightly and reached to the very spot the dart entered and then went limp. She had been stunned with the "zombie" toxin that would leave her confused and disoriented for three days. Enough time to get her to the

French and enough time for them to get her onto the *Lady Giselle* and out to sea.

Admiral Versallies saw the small party approach the Cotonou Lagoon through his binocular from the *Lady Giselle*'s deck as they crossed the flats of sand that intermingled with the seawater.

He could see the party through the morning fog approach the awaiting boat that had been sent to pick up this special cargo. This would weaken King Ghezo's resolve, to have a member of his royal family stolen right under his nose. The king would never dream that Nima was in his possession. But he would soon find out, and it would be absolutely too late to stop the transfer.

As the warriors approached, they carried Nima over their shoulders wrapped in traditional Dahomey cloth, the only thing that would remain with her of her homeland. She lay lifeless over his shoulder but was gingerly placed onto the boat.

Chief Akuna was sent word of the success of the mission. He reveled in the knowledge of how this would affect the household of the king. Once the king knew of the kidnapping of Nima, it would forever change his views on losing someone to slavery.

Chapter 4

They brought him his favorite meal; he pushed the plate away. The women of his household could not please him with anything or anyone. The king was inconsolable after learning of the fate of his Nima. *How could they infiltrate his fortified camp?* he asked himself. He never thought he would see the day when that would happen. He stood up from his mahogany chair adorned with elephant tusks and cushioned with panther skin and paced around his bedroom chamber. He knew that something had to be done quickly to foil the plans of whoever took Nima. The Voodou priests were called, and the people gathered outside. The head priest was a small boney man of medium height with small feet and long yellowing toes. He started the ceremony with the usual reverence for the king. Then he drank palm wine and spat into the fire several times as nightfall had come. The flames sputtered about for a brief moment and went back quickly to fully flicker in twilight. He sang a song, and the people joined in at the appropriate time.

The priest had a powerful baritone voice, and he sang with much vehemence. The people repeated the verses and circled about him. The king stood up, and the people opened the circle and dropped to the ground and placed their hands on the dusty red earth and wailed and cried, letting their tears work into the earth. This went on nonstop for three days. The king also sent out his best trackers to see if they could find some remnant or evidence of where she was; they returned unsuccessful. Before the chanting ended, the household slave that betrayed him was dead, and he knew the enemy that put a hole in his heart.

Chapter 5

Nima lay on the ground near three other women she did not know. They were all chained together, crying bitter tears. All had been transposed from the lives they knew and the people they loved. Husbands unable to rescue them from the deadly trip ahead and fathers unable to shield them from the hard life to come. One woman mumbled incoherently, and another coughed insistently. The air was thick with the smell of the ocean. Nima tried to sit up but felt dizzy. Instead she rested against a wooden post. Nearby, voices arose with urgency.

"High tide is tonight. Let's get our cargo onto the ship." They were being moved, first to a small boat that ten people fit into then to a larger vessel that looked like an elephant atop water to swallow them up and turn them inside out. Into the muddy waters they went; her feet did not want to be released from all she knew. She had to be pulled up and away by harsh white hands.

The French ship was filled to capacity for the journey from Cotonou Lagoon, Benin, to Nice, France.

As the sea captain watched this group of human cargo come on board, he recognized someone familiar among them.

A woman who had spoken his language and who he was certain was part of the royal family of King Ghezo. He ordered his crewmen to bring this woman to his cabin. He would shelter her from the pungent belly below and take what he wanted from her. He would be setting sail within the hour. He cataloged the rest of his cargo: 150 slaves, sixty bolts of cotton, and one hundred pounds of iron ore in the ship's log under the date of July 3, 1847.

Chapter 6

She remembered someone coming into the room and forcing her to drink water and trying to feed her and hearing voices around her as if someone was evaluating her situation. What brought her back to the harsh reality was the cold seawater that was dumped on her. Somehow tasting the saltwater and smelling the sea air broke the haze.

The only saving grace of sorts was that she knew one of her captors. The captain had been at the palace and was received by the king and his court. She had seen him along with his soldiers at the palace at least twice. She knew from her conversations with the king what some of the discussion was about.

The holding area where the others were kept was below deck toward the forward bow. It was a shadowy area that had very little light. This was welcomed so as not to see the full level of denigration there. Of which the poor ventilation made that suffering doubly hard. It reeked of a multitude of foul smells and had to be cleaned twice a day. The sorrow and human humiliation could not be cleared from this place.

Nima had to mentally transform herself back to the place where she was born by closing her eyes to block out what was going on around her. Take herself to her childhood games or thoughts of the rolling farms she visited. The first time she saw a giraffe or tasted bushmeat. Or had her hair braided by her friend using shea butter and fragrant oil. Back home she could girl talk with Zaillia and be scolded by her mother when she ventured too far away from her sight.

As a child, she secretly wanted to be like the Amazon warrior women going on hunting expeditions for game like antelope or water buffalo. She wanted to learn how to throw a spear and prepare for battles. This, of course, was out of the question as a daughter of the king. But it did not stop her from asking him; he would laugh lightly at her request to be a warrior. He would explain that this would not be her destiny and nicknamed her his warrior princess. Nima didn't think it should be so impossible. As she grew older, she better understood the hierarchy.

Nima would feel the pain and loss of never seeing her village again, tasting her favorite meal, or enjoying the touch of her husband. She would not see her child or witness the misty mornings mingle with the fragrant smell of the cooking fires started nearby her door. She would miss much and endure much.

As she stood in the captain's quarters, the wooden walls began to move in on her. The rocking motion and spinning came in on her, and she fainted.

She was awakened by the jolt of smelling salts. Her eyes could hardly focus on the person in front of her. He was speaking and offering water.

The water she wanted, so she drank from the shiny cup, gagging at first. He spoke again.

In French, he said, "Do you want more water?" Nima's response was delayed. She was still trying to keep her head from falling back to the wooden floor. She nodded, and he offered more water; this time she drank the liquid more quickly than before and began to regain her senses.

"What is your name?"

This time his voice boomed, and she shivered as she answered, "Nima." She could see that he was an important man of authority. His clothing was adorned with shiny golden ornaments, and he had a well-kept look about him. His hair was the color of grass in the dry season, and his long nose had small nostrils.

"You will stay here with me, this is my cabin." He went on to say, "You will sleep over there"—pointing to the floor—"or in my bed as I desire it."

He took something off his wooden table and moved toward her again and reached down to unchain her hands. He looked at her wrist with curiosity, turning them over to see if they were free of sores. A knock came to the door.

"Captain, I have food for the wench as you ordered, sir."

"Enter and set it down and leave," he replied.

"This food is for you, do not waste it—EAT!"

Then the captain left the room for his 6:00 a.m. tour. The door slammed shut, and it made a clicking sound.

Nima was alone again. She looked about the cabin and tried to interpret what was there—a lamp, clock, compass. Nima did not have an appetite.

She dreamed of her husband Manko and her homeland. It was six months after their marriage, and he seemed to be troubled. He told her that the white man came ever closer to their lands and continued to demand more slaves. He and his men had to go further into neighboring Nigeria to conduct more raids and bring back captives. He would have to leave soon to lead the army and would be away a long time. That would be the last time she saw him. She reached out to him and held his face to give him a kiss and said, "I will miss you," and he replied, "And I you."

She awoke from the dream suddenly as the rattling noise returned, and the door to the cabin opened. It was the captain returning from his watch. He looked at her briefly and then went to his desk. He saw the uneaten food and spoke to Nima.

"You have not eaten, ah! If you do not, I will have it forced"—he made a gesture with his hands—"down your throat, *you* will eat." He took the tray and placed it in front of her, and she ate.

Two weeks passed. Nima had heard many sounds, hidden in the captain's cabin: the loud voices of the shipmates and cries of women and children and the ocean.

She thought of her dream and if Manko could see what had happened. She had no one to help her now. The captain had shown her a sort of twisted kindness, but like the others, she had been soiled. Her future was uncertain, and her emotions for now had numbed. The day had come for arrival at their berth destination. They arrived at Port Boudex on the western shore of France. The captain noted in his log: "One hundred slaves survived the voyage. Fifty-five males, sixteen females, twenty-nine children."

He prided himself in writing this entry as his cargo was of great monetary reward to him and his crew. He also reported that they arrived ahead of schedule as the winds had added extra time to this voyage. This was always good news to his investors.

The slaves would be transferred quickly to the warehouse. They would be attended to by doctors as several were suffering from dysentery and other ailments. He would have little to do with that but would be kept abreast of events.

Nima was not sure what to expect now that the boat had docked. She waited with the others in the full sun. The men were checking leg irons and getting everyone to their feet. They were pushed into an ox-laden wagon and moved along the waterfront as quickly as possible. People stopped and stared at the Negroes.

The days ahead would spin out of control for Nima. No aspect of her life was her own. She would be inspected by peering eyes and hands as men, fully dressed, looked at her near nakedness. Gawking stares and mental calculation made for the usefulness of strong legs, firm breasts, and good teeth.

Being purchased by French colonist Vernou to work in his home, serving his family would be her fate. Her first day in his home was frightening. The huge building with two stone lions standing at its entryway seemed ready to devour her. She was taken to the back entry and led into a large cooking area. There she met the woman who she would take orders from, Madam Maria Mignon.

This genteel woman, as she was, was a staunch abolitionist and despised the system of slavery. This was unknown to her employer, but became evident in her actions.

Madam Maria Mignon was a petite woman with features that could be set in porcelain. Having been raised in the south of France where the sun reached the skin to tint it creamy white, she was considered a beauty with fiery red hair and intense green eyes. But she lacked the placement in society of becoming a great lady. Her father worked for a winery for most of his life, and her mother had died in labor after the birth of her sister.

She had some education and was able to get employment at this aristocratic home. Her mistress trusted her and depended on her.

The arrival of this newest slave woman was expected. Madam Mignon had planned to use her as a washer and kitchen maid. She would be one of the lucky ones, considering her station.

When Madam Mignon first laid eyes on Nima, she didn't realize how hard it would be to control her emotions. Nima was thin, barely clothed, and shivering from the cold rain.

She was thrown at her by the horsemen and still chained at the hands and feet.

She angrily spoke to the horsemen. "Remove these chains immediately. And why did you not give her a blanket? She'll catch her death in this weather."

The horseman looked surprised at her tone but obeyed. As he fumbled with the keys, Madam Mignon went to get a blanket. Nima stood frozen, not knowing what to do.

When Madam Mignon returned, she wrapped the blanket around Nima and eased her into the kitchen near the fire to warm. The girl looked exhausted. Food was offered in the form of a warm bowl of stew and was eaten quickly.

"You will sleep here by the fire tonight. Tomorrow I will bring you warm clothing and show you your work."

Madam Mignon left Nima to stare at the fire. She could not process this place. All she could do was fall into a fitful sleep. Awaking the next day with a fever, Nima lay flexed, shivering, and sweating. Master Vernou was consulted and came to view the invalid woman slave that he spent time and money on in this unproductive mode. Angrily he exclaimed to Madam Mignon, "How did this occur? This slave has come one thousand miles, and as soon as she enters my door, she collapses?" Madam Mignon tried to explain but was cut off.

"Call Dr. Nivelles, see what he can do for her."

"Yes sir," she replied.

"And make sure he gives me a report. Have any of the others shown signs of illness?"

"No, just this creature."

"See to it." Walking out of the room as he came in—angrily.

Madam Mignon opened the large mahogany door to allow the doctor in and escorted him to the girl.

"Has she eaten or drunk anything since she arrived" he asked.

"No, not since last night. We put her in the cellar and left her food and water. I'm not sure if she took any. She is quite sick, doctor."

His examination would reveal much. She was in a delirious state. Mumbling incoherently and with fever. Unable to speak, the doctor had to deduce and treat her regardless. He had seen this sickness before and knew exactly what to do to get this woman well, even though she would be treated harshly once that happened. He had a plan to save one out of the thousands.

The master had to be told.

"She has a case of scurvy. She must be given fresh food, nothing cured, and plenty of oranges and limes. I've given the instructions to your Madam Mignon."

"Is this household in any danger?"

"No, Monsieur Vernou, you are in no danger."

"Then she will recover?"

"Oh yes, but she might have weakness, and recovery could be long and arduous," he explained.

Dr. Nivelles had to lie to save this woman's life. He was willing to do it, so he told Vernou that she would have to be moved and, ultimately removed, to a warmer climate, no harsh French winters.

"Damn, I am not prepared to house an invalid, Dr. Nivelles!" exclaimed Monsieur Vernou.

"I have not made a dime from this shipment of blacks. I will have to sell her off when she recovers—at a loss."

"Wait, I have an alternative that will bring you income, and then you can send her to your plantation in Guadeloupe. My friend Charles Cordier, the sculptor, needs a model for his ethnic series. He will pay you if the girl poses for him as long as he needs."

"Yes, yes, this is an excellent proposal." Vernou's face changed to reveal agreement and relief.

"Let me contact him. He has just returned to Paris and is a personal friend of mine. He will be excited. I will return in two days to check on the girl and should have an answer for you."

"Until then," replied Monsieur Vernou.

Dr. Nivelles left the Vernou house and returned to his home. The next day, he sent a message to Cordier. The letter explained the situation.

Cordier's prompt affirmative reply was expected. He wrote back with the location of his studio and a date he would be ready to work with Nima.

Chapter 7

Charles Cordier was not your typical celebrated artist. He had trained under Francisco Reede and developed the opulence style that the French aristocrats loved. Charles Cordier was the fourth child of a pharmacist born in the south of France in November 1827. He showed artistic prowess early on and received recognition at the local art school. Young Cordier was five feet five and had curly dark-brown hair receding at the brow line. His hair continued down the sides of his face into a beard, mustache, and goatee. He had attentive brown eyes and a long flat nose that jutted out over his mouth. His hands were strong and with nimble fingers that aided him when working on his masterpieces. He was a traveler, and other parts of the world intrigued him. But what set him apart from his contemporaries was the belief in the human spectrum of beauty. It was early 1847, and he had just returned from southern Spain in search of a wide range of colored marbles that excited him. The trip home to France gave him an opportunity to think about their potential uses. He longed for his studio at the academy. To be able to work the cold stone into a fine bust of some aristocrat would be financially rewarding, but he had other ideas.

He was an indulger of fragmentary ideas. Images as stunning as the stone raced through his head. He would beautify and immortalize the major races of the world in a new way.

Cordier wanted to meet his new specimen as soon as possible. He wondered what her bone structure was like, the contours of her neck, lips, and cheekbones. In his second correspondence to Dr. Nivelles, he inquired into her health and readiness.

> Dear Dr. Nivelles:
>
> What is the nature of this Negro's illness? Obviously I need her well. Also tell me about her features, can she speak French, and can she follow instructions?
>
> > Sincerely,
> >
> > Charles

His reply encouraged Cordier's artistic creativity:

> Dear M. Cordier:
>
> Nima is delicate. I estimate her age to be of nineteen or twenty. Her figure is slight but with erect posture. Her skin is free of pimples or lacerations. The shape of her head is a diamond shape with walnut-sized cheekbones, almond eyes, and full lips. Her recovery has gone well, and I am sure we will be able to send her to you soon. And surprisingly, she speaks a little French. I am sure you will find her a great example of African beauty.
>
> > Cordially,
> >
> > Dr. Nivelles

Upon Dr. Nivelles's return to the Vernou home, he found Nima's recovery had already been established by her master. She was in the root cellar, retrieving vegetable for the day's meals. She appeared to be strong, and Dr. Nivelles asked her how she was feeling.

"I am much better," she answered.

"Are you still taking the drops in water?" he asked.

"Yes," she answered.

Nima realized that he was the medicine man that had helped her and felt safer and less afraid.

"Nima, you will be visiting with my friend soon. He is going to take clay and make a figure of you. You will be safe with him and not work as hard," Dr. Nivelles explained.

Nima didn't understand. Back home, making a figure in clay was a bad thing. It meant witchcraft.

She asked the doctor, "He is a witch doctor, he kill me."

"No, no, you are a jewel to him, he wants to preserve you, show you to the world. Your beauty—he will not harm you, you must trust me," he further explained.

Nima was confused and felt that her beauty could only be appreciated by her own people back home. She will never feel beautiful again among these people.

The next day, she was taken to Cordier's studio. Cordier was well trained in the best art academies of his day. He elevated his skills to attract the very rich patrons to his studio. They wanted massive, decorated, arched sculptures and water fountains. But he was in love with the landscape of beauty outside of France. And he found one such thing in Nima.

When Nima arrived in his studio, he could tell she was afraid. He led her to the fireplace and handed her some wine to soothe her. After a few minutes, he reassured her by saying "Don't be afraid. I will not hurt you. All I want you to do is sit here and be still" as he lead her to that place.

Nima looked around her and tried to make sense of her surroundings. She saw pottery, stone, wooden boxes, tools, and so much more. He sat across from her and started looking at her intently. There was something covered over in cloth near him; he took the covering off and began to press his fingers into it. She watched as he worked his clay, instructively barely moving. Cordier looked at the nearby terra-cotta clay armature and started to sketch on paper his approach. At times he would work between the clay and the pencil drawing, but spent most of the time working the clay. Patting the clay firmly and blending the slabs together with his fingers. Using calipers to take measurements from Nima's face, the space between her chin and hairline, and the room between the ears. Building up her profile and shaping her eyes, lips, and cheeks. Working on the texture of her hair and shape of her neck and shoulders. No detail was missed. He continued working the clay, spinning it around on the turntable, absorbing, reflecting on his subject to capture and depict her every feature. In a short period of time, the sample maquette was completed.

The next step would be to make a plaster mold. Once the clay statue is placed inside the mold, it's allowed to dry, and a layer of wax in poured inside. Next, Cordier will fire the piece in the kiln. Like hot lava from the violent eruptions of a volcano, the 2100-degree bronze is poured into the cast. Melting the waxlike flesh, contouring itself to the mold, and when it cools, what is unmasked is pure beauty.

Nervously, the kiln is opened to reveal the first fired piece of Nima. The piece is then mounted with a wooden base for support. And then the artist can view in 360 degrees his work.

She was outstanding to Cordier. It went beyond him appreciating his own handiwork.

This contribution to the art world was not appreciated by most of his contemporaries. Not seeing beyond their own prejudices was their biggest problem. He knew that this was going to be a companion piece to his *Said Abdullah* bronze. As often happens, your companion steals the moment as no other can.

They would meet in his studio for two months until his work was finished. In reality, he was finished with his sketches and different poses by the third week of their sittings, but extended it.

Cordier wanted to treat her like any other model that sat for him. He viewed her as proof positive of the range of beauty that God had given the world. The fact that he opposed slavery and worked with abolitionists was well-known. He intended to show her beauty to the world and work to abolish slavery in France.

The choice was clear after a restless night of dreaming and a foreboding sense of urgency. After going over his last conversation with Dr. Nivelles, he knew Nima's time with him was complete. She had grown stronger and would be sent on to Monsieur Vernou's plantation in Guadeloupe within weeks.

Cordier was frantic the next day in the studio. When Nima arrived, he looked undone, like the priest back home after his healing chants had exhausted him. His eyes were not connecting with her; they were distant, and it made her feel sad. She had gotten used to his intent gazes and actually wanted to see the image of her that he was creating. She did not know it was the last time they would be together. Cordier knew he had completed the process; there was nothing left to do except show his pieces to the world.

Chapter 8

The morning of January 21, 1848, there was a misty cold rain set over the city. The fine water particles stuck to your skin and stayed with you as you walked into the sanctuary of the Church of Saint-Denis in Paris. The room was filling with the speakers of the day against slavery. There was Jean Lafayette, a half black who had been raised in the West Indies and educated in France as a lawyer. Thankfully, he was an eloquent speaker and used his life as an example. He addressed the group with fervor. Even before he reached the podium, he was sweaty with raw emotions.

My good gentlemen, I stand before you the son of a black woman and a white Frenchman. I never knew my mother. A few days after my birth, she was sent away, sold to some horrid owner miles from where I lay in my rocker. Why my father did this, I am not sure. She had brought to him a son that looked like him, the features she processed where hidden inside the child, not visible to the eye. Yes, I looked like him from the long narrow nose to the dark-brown hair and pale skin complexion. My coloring did not change as time went by. The black part of me remained obscure. But I tell you, sirs, I never forgave my father for such an offense. To sell her and part us was a cardinal sin. I never would know her hand, her kiss on my forehead, her smile as she gently comforted me after a bad dream or tasted her food. Not to know her would shape my life forever.

I am here today to tell you I will never forget that part of me. I am connected to it with unseen strings that reach up into the air and stretch from Nice to her birthland. I will do everything in my power to destroy this system that renders human beings powerless against their own will. Some of you in this room can trace your families back to days of the beautiful sixteenth century. The wine flowed, the weavers made the lovely garments, and the salt mines stored the food. Why did France join in the nasty business of human slavery?

How fine it must be to set your grandson on your knee and talk of your golden days. I too wish to tell my story to my children.

You French have a saying, "Liberty or die." I have heard it many times in the days of the Revolution shouted from the street. Slavery must end, and it must end now.

The next speaker was a wealthy Frenchman named Victor Schoelcher who dedicated his efforts and connections to the abolishment of slavery in France. He started by saying,

I should not be standing here. The French government officially ended involvement in the African slave trade in 1819. Then we officially banned all French citizens from participating in the slave trade in 1831. He picked up several documents and shook it in his hand. Then we signed with Great Britain, Russia, Prussia, and Austria the Quintuple agreement that said ships suspected of carrying slaves could be stopped and searched at sea. Yet the suffering of these people goes on.

The great French abolitionist Victor Schoelcher went on to say,

They are not the savages, we are. We continue to denigrate them. I have traveled the world, opposing slavery. I will not rest until it is truly ended. I oppose our government's involvement in slavery, and I know firsthand the cruelties it produces, may it be done on the island of Guadeloupe or the deep south of the United States. It is our Christian duty to eradicate this vile practice.

Schoelcher concluded.

Chapter 9

The island of Guadeloupe is ruggedly beautiful with lakes, waterfalls, and natural hot springs. When Nima walked off the ship in the port of Basse-Terre, she had little more than the clothes on her back. From the port, she was driven to the Vernou's plantation.

She was glad that she did not suffer during her trip, but felt ill all the same. The strong smell of sugarcane being harvest filled the air and grew stronger as she drew closer to the family home.

She didn't know then the time she would spend there. Nor did she know that her face was about to be looked upon by millions.

The months leading up to the opening ceremony of the Great Exhibition of 1851 flew by. The structure itself was designed by Joseph Paxton, and the project was the brainchild of Prince Albert, husband of the Queen of England. Prince Albert was criticized for undertaking the project. People of the day like

Karl Marx saw the exhibit as an emblem of capitalism for the queen. And others said it was Albertopolis. Now he could stand outside the colossal building and garner much satisfaction from seeing the building finally erected. He could laugh at detractors who said the exhibit was obscure and foolish. *The growing list of participants would quell that reference,* he thought to himself—twelve thousand and counting. In a show of British ingenuity and Victorianism, the 1851 Great Exhibition was nothing short of stunning. The building was a grandiose achievement of iron and glass with gardens and water fountains. Over thirteen thousand exhibitors from all over the world came, and 6.2 million visitors walked through its corridors.

The fifty pieces of the French exhibition had been shipped and set up without incident. The bust of the African Said Abdullah and its companion piece, the *African Venus*, were positioned well. Their debut was exciting for the artist. He had a world stage before him, but even he did not expect the level of interest the two pieces would produce.

One named and the other nameless had caused great stir in the milky landscape of England. Most people had never seen a rendition of African features. The spotlight was shared and sparked further interest from the queen herself. When Cordier was later approached about making a rendition of *African Venus* for the palace, it created quite a stir. Suddenly, anyone who was anyone wanted the *African Venus*.

On opening day, May 1, 1851, Queen Victoria and a crowd of dignitaries and a multitude of people. The list was astonishing and included Americans like Charles Darwin, Samuel Colt, and George Elliot.

The ribbon was cut, and speeches were spoken, and the champagne flowed in the reception hall. Then the people spread out into the vast hallways. Among the things displayed was the Koh-i-noor five-hundred-karat diamond from India, a water fountain of eau de cologne, a single lump of gold from Chile weighing three hundred pounds, and the *African Venus*.

The queen's itinerary was carefully planned out. When she stopped at the French exhibit and whispered to Prince Albert, the crowd clamored. Of course, she could choose anything represented in this Exhibition. There was so much to see it could not be done in one day. She herself would visit more than once and make several purchases.

Along the eastern nave of the Great Exhibition, across from the two white stallions, was the submission of Charles Cordier, the ethnographic sculptor's exhibit. The bust caused controversy as it was part of the French exhibition and the fact that the faces were not European. The newspapers had a field day.

"What vision of beauty is this—a black with a mop for hair and bulging lips" wrote the *London Gazette*.

Another wrote such negative comments, it spurred more visits. When it was reported that Queen Victoria purchased a cast of Nima's bust for her personal collection, the naysayers and the English aristocrats took notice.

By the time the exhibit closed in mid-October 1851, Cordier was getting recognitions from his peers and artistic societies that he did not anticipate, and orders for the *African Venus* were pouring in.

Back home in France, a long-overdue recognition came from the Academy of the Arts. On the night of the awards ceremony, as the red, white, and blue ribbon with golden medallion was placed over his head by Dr. Nivelles, the two men's eyes locked for that split second. They knew what needed to be done.

Chapter 10

Nima worked as kitchen help most of her days at the mansion. There was food to prepare for the household of Vernou and the other entrapped humans. The only thing she could look forward to was learning lacework. She would sit with Justine, who was a lady's maid, for as long as light permitted and watch and learn her handiwork. Once she learned the basics, she became very good. It reminded her of the intimacies that she once had. The delicate balances that had been destroyed were somehow strangely soothed with the working of the lace.

Justine had stories to tell about how the patterns for her work came about. Justine's stories were never too long.

This lace pillowcase pattern was made by me one stormy night. I sit by my window, waiting for my love to come home. He be out on the sea, fishing, and this powerful storm come and make the sky gray and dark, and then the rain and wind come. The raindrops kept coming and hitting the glass pane. So I work my needle

to forget that loud storm. I work in nice pretty flowers
and french knots and scalloped edges.

Nima could remember the colorful appliqué flags and
designs from her homeland and started using them in her work.
The emblem on the Royal Palace buildings she transferred onto
pillowcases and added new elements to it. She named it point to
point.

The letters written to Monsieur Vernou went unanswered
for several weeks. Dr. Nivelles and Cordier were told that he was
traveling abroad on business and was unsure of his return date.
Madame Mignon was contacted and confirmed that Vernou was
in Guadeloupe.

The trip to Guadeloupe would take one month, but Cordier
was willing to go. Once there, he would convince Vernou to
release her.

"She deserves to be free," Cordier simply but firmly said to M.
Vernou. "Not because of the statue—it's a matter of helping one
to free one," Cordier continued.

"You talk nonsense, Cordier! You have benefited from her,
and now you just say set her free, that is not your decision to
make. You have traveled here for nothing," Vernou scoffed at
him.

Cordier could see he was not getting through to him and
reached into his breast pocket and handed Vernou a wax-sealed
letter.

"What's this?" Vernou asked and began to open it.

"It's a letter from Dr. Nivelles for you."

Vernou snatched the letter from his fingers and used the
letter opener from his fine French desk to open it.

Dear M. Vernou:

Apparently, you have not agreed to free Nima, and this letter was held in case of that. I must break with my oath of silence in the matter of your illegal shipments of slaves and the guns that are on their way to Africa now. You tell the people of France that you hold no slaves, and yet you have run perhaps thousands to your plantation. Nima is yet one that we can save. You do not want your full doings to be exposed in the newspapers or in a well-placed letter from me to our minister of defense. Sign the needed papers and let her leave, and we will not refer to this again.

Cordially,

Dr. Nivelles

Chapter 11

With the financial help of Cordier and Dr. Nivelles and in the company of Madam Mignon, Nima had settled in New Orleans a free person. She lived among other freed blacks in Pointe Coupee, Natchitoches, in the business district. Her apartment was above the dress shop she and Madam Mignon ran together.

Nima thought to herself what this new land of freedom would really mean to her. She was reminded of home almost every day now. Every day, their smiling faces protruded through the door with the ring of the bell of her shop. She could see traces of her people in their walk, talk, and dress. Even when she went two streets over to buy her lunch on occasion, she would taste the flavors in the okra soup. The flavors of home transported her. And she could see them in the blue indigo fabric they wrapped around their heads.

She felt she could be happy here, making pretty things to wear and earning a living as a dressmaker. She had crossed enough oceans and been uprooted enough. This place will end her desultory travels.

She felt her voice return and the possibilities open up before her.

Edwards Brothers Malloy
Thorofare, NJ USA
July 25, 2013